AMBER BROWN
GOES FOURTH

Paula Danziger

AMBER BROWN
GOES FOURTH

Illustrated by Tony Ross

G. P. PUTNAM'S SONS

NEW YORK

Text copyright © 1995 by Paula Danziger
Illustrations copyright © 1995 by Tony Ross
All rights reserved. This book, or parts thereof, may not be reproduced
in any form without permission in writing from the publisher.
G. P. Putnam's Sons, a division of The Putnam & Grosset Group,
200 Madison Avenue, New York, NY 10016.
G. P. Putnam's Sons, Reg. U.S. Pat. & Tm. Off.
Published simultaneously in Canada.
Printed in the United States of America.
Book designed by Donna Mark and Marikka Tamura.
Lettering by David Gatti. Text set in Bembo.

Library of Congress Cataloging-in-Publication Data
Danziger, Paula, 1944– Amber Brown goes fourth / by Paula Danziger. p. cm.
Summary: Entering fourth grade, Amber faces some changes in her life
as her best friend moves away and her parents divorce.
[1. Friendship—Fiction. 2. Divorce—Fiction. 3. Schools—
Fiction.] I. Title. PZ7.D2394A1 1995
[Fic]—dc20   94-41935 CIP AC
ISBN 0-399-22849-7
1   3   5   7   9   10   8   6   4   2
First Impression

To Earl and Shirley Binin
who taught me to celebrate creativity
and individuality

AMBER BROWN
GOES FOURTH

Chapter
One

"You're the kid who has to put her right shoe on before her left." The salesman comes up to me with the foot-measuring thing.

"Yup." I nod. "You remember!"

"How can I forget?" The salesman puts my right foot into the measurer. "The one time I didn't do it your way, you refused to get any shoes . . . . and you accused me of ruining your day . . . . and you threatened to report me to the Society for the Prevention of Cruelty to Children Who Need to Put Their Right Shoe On Before Their Left."

I hold out my right foot and wonder why he's acting like that's so strange. I'm sure that I'm not the only person in the whole entire world who likes to have some things done a certain way. With the way my life goes, it's nice to be sure of some things . . . and I'm sure that I like to put my right shoe on before my left. It makes me feel weird if my left shoe goes on first. In fact, it messes up my entire day.

A little kid comes over and grabs my foot, the left one.

"Foot," she says.

Her mother picks her up. "Sorry she's bothering you. She's learning the names for body parts."

I'm glad that the foot is the part of the body she decided to name.

All around us there are kids . . . . trying on shoes . . . . blowing up balloons . . . . . yelling, "I want those"; "I hate those."

One kid is throwing a temper tantrum

2

because his mother won't buy him sandals for school.

The salesman continues, "And you've got that very colorful name."

I sigh.

My mother looks at her watch.

He thinks for a minute. "Ebony Black. . . . . No, that's not it. Pearl White. No."

"AMBER BROWN," I remind him, "and I don't like to be teased about it."

"Isn't there another family that you always come in with to buy shoes for the new school year?" he asks. "With two little boys, one about your age?"

"They've moved away," my mother says softly.

All of a sudden, I get this empty feeling inside of me.

This will be the first time in my life that I'll be starting school without my best friend, Justin Daniels.

I try not to think about it.

I've been trying not to think about it all summer, especially since I got back from England with my aunt Pam.

My mother puts her hand on mine. "She'd like to see the sneakers with the rhinestones on them."

The man puts down the measurer and looks up information on a card file. "She's grown. Up another shoe size. . . . . Oh, well . . . . it could have been worse. She

could have grown another foot. Then you'd have to buy three shoes." He laughs at his own joke. "Just a little shoe-business humor."

As he goes to the back of the store, he sings, "There's no business like shoe business."

I look at my mother.

She looks at me and shrugs. "The shoes are good quality and cheaper here than the other store. I know he drives you nuts . . . but think what you would be like if you had to be with children and their feet all day."

"It would be a real feat." I giggle.

"You would have to put your heart into it, body and soles."

We both start to laugh.

By the time the guy comes back, my mother and I are both singing, "There's no business like shoe business."

He joins in.

I try on my new shoes.

They're perfect.

My mother smiles at me. "New clothes. New shoes. All ready for a brand-new school year. Fourth grade, get ready for Amber Brown."

I think about what she's just said.

Not only does fourth grade need to get ready for me. . . . I need to get ready for it.

I think of how Justin and I used to pretend that we were knights.

Before we would go off to slay dragons, one of us would yell, "THE BRAVE KNIGHTS GO FORTH!"

To get ready for my new grade, I'm going to have to say to myself, AMBER BROWN GOES FOURTH.

It's not going to be easy without Justin.

Chapter Two

Sitting on my bed, I look at my "Dad Book." It's filled with pictures of my father alone, of him with me, with pictures of the three of us—Mom, Dad, and me. There are even some pictures of just the two of them, before they decided to separate.

Since my mother doesn't like to have pictures of my father around the house, I made up the Dad Book.

If I ever get to visit my dad in France, I've decided to make up a "Mom Book" to take with me. Something tells me that he doesn't have pictures of her around his apartment.

He does have pictures of me though. He told me that when he came over to England to see me when I got chicken pox and couldn't go to him.

Sometimes I talk to the book as if my dad is really here.

Today is one of those days.

"I'm a little nervous about school starting. It's going to be the first time that you're not here for the first day of school. And Justin's not here either."

I look at the picture of my dad, which was

taken when we went to Great Adventure. He's grinning . . . . . . and he's got a piece of cotton candy stuck on his nose.

He can't say anything.

I continue, "Actually, I'm more than just a little nervous . . . I'm scared. Fourth grade . . . . that's supposed to be pretty hard . . . . and Mr. Cohen's not going to be my teacher this year. . . . What if my brain is so filled with everything from nursery school, kindergarten, first, second, and third grade that I don't have room in it to put any new facts? What if I get a desk that wobbles? Or a desk that some dumb kid sat in last year and there's still some dumb kidness on the desk that's going to rub off on me?" I can almost hear my father laugh as I say that.

It even makes me smile . . . . . a little . . . and then I continue, "What if nobody wants to be my best friend? Daddy, I'm really out of practice for making best friends. I haven't had to do it since preschool—and I didn't even have to think about it then."

Then I give the picture a kiss.

I can almost taste the cotton candy on his nose. "And Daddy, this is the big news: Mommy is going out with this guy named Max. She started going out with him while I was in England. And I think she really likes him. And she says that he really likes her."

I look at the picture of my father.

He's still smiling.

I'm not. "When I got back, Mommy wanted me to meet Max, but I didn't want to."

I think about how I don't want her to have a boyfriend, not unless it's my dad. When she told me all about him, I got really upset and I really cried, not make-believe-to-try-to-get-my-own-way tears, but real tears. So then she said that I don't have to meet him for a while, not unless it gets VERY serious.

I start talking to the picture of my dad

again. "This could get VERY serious, Dad. If you are thinking about coming back to us, you better do it soon. I'm getting worried.

Max doesn't even live here. He lives in a whole different town. What if Mommy and Max decide to get married? Then you and Mommy won't be able to be married. What if they decide to move to his town . . . . and what if I have to go to a different school?"

My father says nothing.

Maybe I should call him and talk to the real person, not just his picture.

But then I don't think I could say all of this to him really . . . . . or to my mother . . . . or to anyone.

"How does this look?" My mother walks into my room.

I close my Dad Book, turn it upside down, and look at her.

She's wearing a black skirt, a raspberry-colored blouse, and jewelry.

Actually, she looks really pretty, but I'm not sure I want to tell her that.

I sniff the air. "You've got a lot of perfume on."

Then I scrunch my nose up.

Actually, she smells good, but I don't want to tell her that either.

She adds a black belt to the outfit and looks in my full-length mirror.

Then she looks at me. "What time is What's His Face picking you up?" I ask.

"MAX is picking me up any minute." She gives me a look.

"What time will you be home?" I take a strand of hair and start to chew on it.

"I'm not sure, but, honey, you don't have to worry. Joanie said that she'll spend the night. And I'll be home long before you wake up in the morning."

I continue to chew on my hair. "Maybe I won't go to sleep until you come back."

My mother sighs. "It's going to be very late."

"I'll wait up."

She tries to change the subject. "Honey, please don't chew on your hair. You know how Aunt Pam's cat, Chesire, is always coughing up hair balls and leaving them all over the place. I'm afraid that you're going to start doing that."

She points to a corner and teases, "You know, little Amber hair balls everywhere."

Even though I think it's funny, I don't smile. "I'll stay awake until you get home. So don't stay out too late."

She looks like she's going to give me a lecture, but then all she says is, "Okay."

I know that she's sure that I'll fall asleep, but I won't.

I know I won't.

Chapter
Three

I'm not going to get out of bed.

Not today.

Not tomorrow.

Not for entire school year, which starts today.

It was hard getting out of bed yesterday and listening to Mom after her big date with Max.

She likes him, really likes him.

She says that she's sure that I'm really going to like him, too.

I'm sure that I really won't.

I don't ever want to meet him.

I don't ever want to like him.

I'm very sure that I won't.

And I'm also sure that I don't want to get out of bed and go to school.

My alarm clock oinks at me.

Actually, it's a combination piggy bank and alarm clock.

It's a pig taking a bubble bath, a present from Aunt Pam.

When I put money in, it snorts and thanks me.

When the alarm goes off, it oinks.

I push down the button, stop the alarm, and put a pillow over my head.

In about four minutes, the Mom Alarm pulls the pillow off my head to wake me up.

This alarm is a real person who rumples my hair and says different things depending on the day.

After her date with Max, she woke me up saying, "I told you that you would fall asleep."

Today, Mom Alarm pulls the pillow off my head and says, "Wake up, darling. . . . It's the first day of school."

There's no button to turn the Mom Alarm off.

Opening my eyes just enough to sort of see her, I say, "Fourth grade's not so important. Wake me up this time next year and I'll think about fifth grade."

My mother tickles me. "Get showered. Get dressed. Be downstairs in half an hour to get a nutritious, yummy breakfast. Then I'll drive you to school."

"I can walk to school. You haven't had to drive me there for two years."

I think about how I used to walk to and

from school with Justin. Then after school, I used to stay at his house until my mom came home.

Now everything has changed.

I repeat, "Mom, I can walk to school."

My mother sighs. "We've already had this discussion. I don't want you to walk there alone, so I'll drive you to school, and at the end of the day I'll pick you up after Elementary Extension."

I put the pillow over my head.

Elementary Extension. It's this special program for kids who can't go home right after school.

It's all Justin's father's fault. If he hadn't gotten that stupid new job, all our lives wouldn't have had to change.

I wonder if Justin's mom is waking him up right now too.

And I wonder if he's thinking about how different it's going to be for him . . . . and if he's missing me, too.

"Rise and shine, my darling daughter." My mom pulls the pillow off my head and uses her voice that says "Now get out of bed if you wish to remain my darling daughter."

She also starts tickling my feet.

I, Amber Brown, do not like to have my feet tickled.

In fact, I hate it.

So I get out of bed, tripping over my new school notebook.

Picking up the notebook, I put it next to my pencil box.

I've decorated the box with all sorts of stickers and filled it with pens, pencils, and erasers.

Taking my shower, I think about a lot of things. . . . . What will my new teacher be like? Which desk will I sit in? Who will sit next to me? Will Hannah Burton still be mean to me? Will some of the boys still be so immature? Will there be any new kids in the class who will need a new friend?

I get out of the shower, dry off, and brush my teeth and my hair (not with the same brush).

Clothes.

I put on black leggings and a long T-shirt that Aunt Pam bought me this summer. It's got a map of the London underground, their subway, on it. I've never worn it, saving it for the first day of school.

On go my new shoes, right shoe first and then the left.

I wonder if Justin is putting on his shoes right now.

I wonder if he remembers to lace them or if he's going to trip because I'm not there to remind him to lace them . . . or if someone else will remind him.

My notebooks and writing stuff go into my new flourescent-pink knapsack, along with the good-luck troll that Aunt Pam gave me a couple of years ago.

I hear the phone ring.

Then it stops.

"Amber," my mother calls up the steps, "it's for you. Your father. Hurry up."

I rush to the phone.

My father is calling from Paris, France.

"Daddy!" I pick up the phone, out of breath.

I hear the click as my mother hangs up the downstairs phone.

"Amber." My father's voice sounds so close even though I know how far away he is. "I just wanted to call to wish you a happy first day of school. I only wish I could be there with you."

"With us?" I keep hoping that means that he and Mom will get back together, even though they keep telling me that they won't.

"Amber." My father sighs. "Honey, not there, not in that house . . . . I need a place of my own."

We are both silent for a few minutes, and then I say, "I miss you, Daddy."

"I miss you too. I wish I could see what you're wearing right now and be there later to hear all about your day. Around six o'clock your time, I'll call to find out how everything went."

I figure that out. . . . . That's midnight his time.

Before hanging up, we have a kissing contest . . . . . making fast kissing sounds until one of us gets tired lips. As usual, I win.

When we hang up, I feel really glad that he remembered and called, and really sad that he isn't living closer.

Going downstairs, I think more about this being my first day.

I wish that it were this time tomorrow so that I will have already gotten through my first day of school and know that everything has gone well.

I wish that my new teacher is wonderful and thinks that I'm wonderful.

I wish that I didn't feel so nervous.

I wish.

Chapter Four

I, Amber Brown, think that the school playground should be renamed. It should be called the school hang-around-and-talk ground, at least for the older kids . . . . like the fourth graders on up . . . . at least for the first day of school.

While we've been talking, I've been looking around. So far, there are no new fourth graders. So far, everyone who was best friends last year are best friends this year.

No best friend vacancies so far . . . . . except for me.

"Amber, what did you do over the summer?" Alicia Sanchez asks me.

"I went to England."

"Name dropper." Hannah Burton makes a face at me. "Name dropper," she repeats, sticking her nose up in the air. "You're just trying to impress everyone."

That's not fair. Alicia asked me what I did, and I told her. I went to England.

"And what did you do over the summer?" Naomi Schwartz asks Hannah.

"My family rented a house at the Jersey shore. That's where I got this great tan." She tries to look like a model.

I pretend to yawn.

"Where's Brandi?" Alicia Sanchez asks. "Didn't she visit you at the shore?"

"Yeah, but that was at the beginning of the summer. I don't know what she's doing right now . . . . and actually, I don't care." Hannah shrugs. "She and her family are still in California, I think. I don't know."

26

"I thought you were best friends," Alicia says. "How come you don't know?"

Hannah shrugs again but says nothing.

I guess that Hannah has a best-friend vacancy too, but the way she acts I don't want to even be her worst friend, let alone her best friend. She's such a monster, she should have a best FIEND.

"I hear that you got chicken pox in London," Tiffany says to me.

I nod. "On the second day. . . . Can you believe it?"

Hannah Burton interrupts and says, "I got chicken pox in the first grade."

"Disease dropper." I make a face.

"You are just so immature." Hannah sticks her nose up in the air. "You are such a dweeb. Back from England . . . . . Her Dweebness."

"Watch it. If you keep your nose up like that and it rains, you could drown. Not that anyone would care."

Gregory Gifford pretends to talk into a television microphone. "And there you have it, sports fans. Round one of the rematch between Brown and Burton. Some say it is going to be the fight of the century. Some say it's just the beginning of another school year."

"I didn't start it." I glare at Hannah, who is wearing a shirt that says, MY PARENTS WENT TO THE JERSEY SHORE AND ALL I GOT WAS THIS STUPID T-SHIRT.

Personally, I think her shirt should say, MY PARENTS GOT MARRIED AND ALL THEY GOT WAS THIS STUPID KID.

Jimmy Russell and Bobby Clifford come running.

They begin making rude noises with their armpits.

After making a really gross noise with his armpit, Jimmy announces that they are planning a Burping Olympics and everyone can sign up after lunch.

29

"Let me find my pen." I cross my eyes.

"I can't wait." Naomi giggles and makes a gagging motion.

Bobby burps and then says, "You can make fun all you want. We're going to be giving away a really great prize."

"I can't wait to hear this." Naomi shakes her head.

"Ta-da." Jimmy holds up a make-believe trophy. "We're giving away the musical mermaid that I gave my sister last Christmas."

"She hated it," Bobby tells us.

"It was on sale, very cheap." Jimmy laughs.

"It's so ugly." Bobby laughs.

"She gave it back to me for my birthday. So now it's going to be our burping trophy. We'll bring it in tomorrow," Jimmy promises.

They start making rude body noises and burping sounds.

The rest of the boys join in.

Some things never change.

Last year the boys made monkey sounds.

This year it's burping sounds.

Last year Fredrich Allen was picking his nose and chewing it.

This year he's still doing it.

I know because some of the boys just yelled to him, "Hey, pick me a winner."

Some things have changed, though. Tiffany Shroeder's name. It's now Tiffani, and she got a bra over the summer and actually needs it.

Jimmy and Bobby tried to snap the back of her bra when we came into school.

Mr. Cohen, our last year's teacher, made them stop.

Another change that I can't help thinking about again is that Justin isn't here for the first day of school for the first time in six years, since preschool.

I bet that Justin could have won the burping contest. Justin can even burp the entire alphabet backward and forward.

Gregory Gifford is playing sportscaster again. "It's Freddie Romano in the lead . . . . . with forty-two consecutive burps."

"Thank you, sports fans." Freddie pretends to bow to a huge audience. "I owe my success to the two cans of soda that I had for breakfast."

The school bell rings.

It's time for class to begin.

I wonder what our new teacher is going to be like.

I wonder what class is going to be like without Justin.

I wonder where I've put my knapsack.

Chapter
Five

"Amber, congratulations. You are the first person this year to use the lost and found." Mrs. Peters, the school secretary, smiles at me, holding on to my pink knapsack.

"Have you lost anything else, dear?" she asks.

I want to say, "Yes. . . . My best friend. . . . . Has anyone turned one in?"

I just stand there.

She reminds me, "You better get to class, Amber. You're late."

I look at the clock.

I'm late for the first day of fourth grade.

Grabbing my knapsack, I yell, "Thanks," and rush down the hall.

Mr. Robinson, the principal, stops me, makes me go halfway back and walk slowly.

Then he yells at me for being late.

I quickly walk to class, passing the third-grade room.

Mr. Cohen is introducing himself to his new class.

They are sooooooo lucky.

I rush into the fourth grade classroom.

"You're late." Hannah Burton looks at her watch.

"Thank you, Big Ben." I call her by the name of the large clock in London and look for a place to sit.

Looking around the room, I see that

everyone is sitting in the same rows that they were in last year, the same seats.

I sit down in what would have been my old desk in this new classroom.

The desk next to me is empty.

"Welcome, Amber." The teacher smiles at me. "My name is Mrs. Holt, and Tiffani explained that you were looking for your knapsack. I see that you've found it."

I look up at our teacher and smile back. "Hi."

Mrs. Holt is a new teacher.

I don't know what happened to the old fourth-grade teacher.

Anyway, Mrs. Holt is not only new, she's very pretty, with brown eyes, brown skin, and brown hair. Her eyelashes are the longest I've ever seen.

She's wearing a long purple skirt and a beautiful pink top.

I hope that she's as good a teacher as Mr. Cohen . . . . and as nice.

Passing out notecards, Mrs. Holt tells us to fill in all of the important information.

NAME

ADDRESS

PARENT(S) OR GUARDIAN(S) NAMES

WHAT WOULD YOU LIKE TO TELL ME
ABOUT YOURSELF?

WHAT WOULD YOU LIKE TO LEARN
THIS YEAR?

WHAT WOULD YOU LIKE TO HAVE HAPPEN
THIS YEAR?

The first two are easy.

I definitely know my name and address.

For my parents' names, I think about putting MOMMY and DADDY, but decide against it.

I don't want Ms. Holt to think I'm a jokester right away.

She already knows that I'm a knapsack-loser.

I put down my parents' real names, Sarah and Phil.

The rest is not so easy.

What should I tell her about me?

After doodling on a piece of paper for a few minutes, I write on the notecard:

About me— I don't know what to say. Couldn't you have made this a true / false
question . . . or multiple choice?

The other questions are a little easier.

I guess I want to learn more about people. ~~Some days~~ I don't really understand ~~them~~.
And I want to find out if there are any secret, major ways to make a new best friend.
What would I like to have happen this year? That's easy. I want my parents to get back together again, for Justin and his family to move back to make another good friend to have as back-up, in case Justin ever had to leave again.

Looking at the last answer, I hope that Ms. Holt doesn't think that I only think about myself, so I add . . . .

...... and peace on earth, no more pollution, no more world hunger.

Then I think of one more thing that I
want, and add . . . .

*I would like it if all the
brussels sprout crops failed this year.*

Finding the notecard, I put it on the side
of my desk and wait for something exciting
to happen.

Chapter Six

2,672 divided by 12.

Why is Mrs. Holt doing this to me?

"Knock knock." Someone raps on the classroom door.

"Who's there?" Jimmy Russell calls out.

"Orange." Bobby Clifford turns to him.

"Orange who?" Jimmy grins at him.

"Orange you glad that we're in the fourth grade now?"

Mrs. Holt gives them the special half smile–half frown teacher look. "Gentlemen, that was the door, not an excuse to tell a joke."

Mrs. Holt walks over and opens the door.
In walks Mrs. Clarke, the vice-principal.
And she's not alone.

"I just thought it would be nice to show
Brandi to her new classroom and see how
you all are doing." She smiles.

Practically everyone in the class looks at Brandi Colwin, starts waving, and calls out stuff like "Welcome Back," and "I love your hair."

I smile at her and wave.

I like the way she looks.

She's wearing purple leggings, a long T-shirt with lots of rhinestones on it, and pink sneakers with sparkly laces.

Her long, blond, curly hair has something special in it.

It's hard to tell from this far away, but I can see that it's special.

Mrs. Holt says, "Welcome, Brandi."

A beeper sounds from somewhere in the room.

Mrs. Clarke goes into her purse and pulls out a walkie-talkie.

It beeps at her again.

She answers, listens for a minute, and then says, "He did WHAT?"

Everyone looks at her.

She says, "Excuse me, please."

And then she walks out the door.

Brandi is just standing there, looking around the room.

I really like her new look.

Mrs. Holt says, "Now, Brandi . . . . let's find you a seat."

I decide that I better do something fast, so I yell out, "There's an empty seat next to me!"

"She didn't raise her hand." Hannah Burton tells on me.

Mrs. Holt looks at her. "Nor did you, Hannah."

Hannah pouts.

I smile.

"Brandi, you may sit next to Amber." Mrs. Holt points to the empty seat next to me. "And Amber, next time remember to raise your hand."

I raise my hand.

She nods.

"Thank you," I say.

Brandi sits down next to me.

Hannah turns and makes a face at us.

Mrs. Holt says, "Amber, show Brandi what we're doing while I get her a set of books."

I show her the math book.

Brandi looks down at my work. "The answer is two hundred twenty-two and two thirds."

"Thanks." I look at her and grin.

Mrs. Holt brings over Brandi's books.

While they talk, I look at Brandi.

Her blond hair has three strands all woven with different colors of string and with three beads on each one . . . one at the top and two at the bottom. Two of the sections start at the top of her head and end at the bottom of her hair. The third one starts at the back of her ear and is about two inches longer than her hair.

Mrs. Holt returns to the front of the room, writes our math assignment on the blackboard, and gives us time to begin our homework.

Before starting, I write a note to Brandi.

Hi. Welcome back. I really love your hair .... and your new look.

I sign it with the special signature I've practiced for someday when I become famous, and then pass it to Brandi.

She reads it, writes something on it, and passes it back to me.

Hi.
Thanks.
And I love your T-shirt and your shoes.

She's got it signed with her own special signature, too.

I think I'm going to have a new best friend.

I write back to her.

I am SO glad that you are back—and sitting next to me.

You know, Justin used to help me with my math ... and I used to help him with his spelling. I can help you with yours too.

                                 amber

Brandi looks at my note, smiles, and then frowns.

She writes on the paper and then passes it back to me.

*I AM a good speller ... ...
... ... and I'm NOT Justin.*

I look at her.
She is staring straight ahead.
"Brandi," I whisper.
She whispers back, "I am NOT Justin."

Mrs. Holt says, "Amber. Brandi. Quiet, or I'm going to have to separate you."

Fourth grade just went from worse to even worse . . . . and it's only the first day.

Chapter Seven

Four days of fourth grade and I, Amber Brown, don't want to go forth. I just want to stay home.

So far, I've had mumps, measles, another case of chicken pox, a sore throat that went all the way down to my toenails, a heart attack, headaches, and food poisoning.

So far, my mother has made me go to school anyway.

My mom is no pushover.

I just don't want to go to school.

It's not that it's SO bad.

Mrs. Holt is a good teacher. She's just not Mr. Cohen.

The kids in the class are fine . . . . all except for Hannah Burton, but that's no different from last year.

And I like Brandi, even though I don't think she likes me very much.

I just miss Justin.

I, Amber Brown, think everyone in the world should have a best friend.

I walk around the playground at recess, silently taking the "Justin tour."

Passing by the swings, I think about how in the first grade we used to take turns pushing each other and pretending that we were birds. We would yell, "Dodo birds . . . . doo doo."

Walking by the jungle gym, I remember how Justin and I organized our kindergarten class to compete in the Jungle Gymboree Olympics. I won a blue ribbon for hanging upside down the longest time while singing the Sesame Street song.

By the water fountain, I remember the time we were studying whales, and Justin and I filled our mouths with water and pretended to be whales with hiccups. We got very wet.

Near the hopscotch area, I remember the time I fell and Justin helped me get the pebble out of my knee.

I think about the time Justin organized our third-grade class, at Halloween, to all scream at once to our teacher, "Mr. Cohen, Mr. Cohen." Justin said that we were "I scream Cohens."

I stand under the tree and look at everyone on the playground.

It looks like most of them have a special friend.

The tree is a special place.

It's where I told Justin that my parents

were getting a divorce and how bad I felt about it.

He didn't say much to help me, but just being able to tell someone helped.

There's no one in my class that I can tell how I feel . . . . or have that much fun with.

I really miss Justin.

Brandi walks slowly past me.

I want to call out to her and ask her to join me, but I don't.

She looks back as if she's going to say something but she doesn't.

I turn away from her as the bell rings.

Recess and the Justin tour are over.

I sure hope that things are going to get better soon.

Chapter Eight

I, Amber Brown, want to declare the first week of school a "do-over," like when you mess up at some sports thing and get to start again at the beginning.

If I could just snap my fingers and yell, "Do-over," there are a couple of things that I would do very differently.

I would not mention Justin to Brandi . . . . . . especially not in a comparing way.

I would try not to care so much that she doesn't seem to want to be my friend.

I would try to just be happy that most of the kids are friendly . . . . . not to be so unhappy that I don't have a best friend . . . and that I don't know how to make one.

I would not show up for the first day at Elementary Extension. Since my name wasn't even on the list, I could have hidden out in the bathroom or something until my mother picked me up.

But now I'm on the list and I've got to sit there with a group of kids from kindergarten through sixth grade. I think they should change the name from Elementary Extension to Kids Being Held Captive in the Cafeteria Waiting for a Grownup to Pick Them Up.

I would try not to think about all of the things that are bugging me . . . . my parents getting a divorce, Justin and his family so far away, Max so near.

But even if it would work to snap my fingers and yell, "Do-over," it would never work.

First of all, I can't even snap my fingers

. . . . . . Instead of the snap sound, I make a sort of thwip sound.

And second, I, Amber Brown, know that just wanting something a whole lot doesn't mean that I'm going to get it.

And I hate knowing that.

"Amber," my mother calls up the stairs. "Supper time."

I walk to the steps and call down, "In a minute."

Washing my hands, I continue to think about all of the stuff that's driving me nuts.

On the way downstairs, I practice snapping my fingers.

Thwip. Thwip. Thwip.

I go into the dining room.

Usually we eat at the kitchen table, but tonight Mom said we should do something special . . . . . take some time for ourselves to talk and hang out.

She's so busy now. Because she has to leave work early to pick me up, she has more work to do at home.

I look at the three place settings on the table.

I thought it was going to be just the two of us.

Maybe she's asked Max to dinner.

I thought she said that she was going to wait a little while before she brought him over to the house.

I, Amber Brown, must find out the answer before I get very upset.

"Mom!" I yell. "Who else is coming to dinner?"

"No one. Just the two of us," she calls out from the kitchen.

Again, I look at the table . . . . three plates . . . . three knives . . . . . . three forks . . .

three spoons . . . . . three napkins . . . three glasses.

It looks like three to me.

I stand there wondering.

Does my mother have an imaginary playmate?

Has Max turned invisible, and is this their way of him being in the house without my having to see him?

Is my mother getting old-timers' disease?

Are my eyes getting bad and am I seeing triple or double plus one?

Have I turned into a major worrier and is there some regular reason for three of everything?

My mother walks into the room, puts down the bowl of spaghetti, and says, "I don't believe it."

She picks up the extra setting, puts it away, and again says, "I don't believe it."

She talks to herself as if I'm not even

there. "I just set the table for the three of us . . . . Phil, me, and Amber . . . as if nothing's changed."

I tug at her sleeve. "Maybe that means you want to get back together again with Daddy."

She shakes her head. "No, it just means that I'm tired and just wasn't thinking. For a long time, the table was set for three, and I guess I just did it again, out of habit."

Getting very quiet, she sits down at the table.

I sit down too. "That's kind of like when I start going over to Justin's old house, or when I pick up the phone to call his old number."

She nods and smiles. "I guess it's all part of our history and we don't always remember that it's not part of our present, at least not in the same way."

I, Amber Brown, think I am too young to

have a history . . . . especially one with so much sad stuff in it.

I remember when everything was fun and easy.

I hope that isn't history.

I look at my mother.

She looks sad and tired.

I know how I feel.

"Mom, let's have a spaghetti-slurping contest."

She laughs. "Amber, I'm a grownup. Grownups don't have spaghetti-slurping contests."

I make a silly face at her.

She laughs.

"Oh please, oh please, oh please," I beg.

She shakes her head, laughs again, and then nods.

We measure out spaghetti strands and then we slurp.

I win.

"The best out of three." My mother has a
line of spaghetti sauce on her chin.

We slurp again.

This time, she wins.

A third slurp . . . . and Amber
Brown is champion.

I look at my mother's face. . . . . It is a grinning, spaghetti sauce–messy face.

"Can you teach me to snap my fingers?" I ask, and show her how I make the thwip sound.

"Nothing to it." She snaps her fingers.

We practice.

Soon I am making a sort of thwip-snap sound.

It's not perfect, but I'm getting there.

When I learn to do it perfectly, I'm going to snap my fingers and say, "Do-over."

If it doesn't work, I'm going to say, "Keep On Going."

I, Amber Brown, am going to get through all of this.

Thwip.

Snap.

Chapter Nine

Elementary Extension.

Every afternoon, it's Elementary Extension . . . . . . the same old thing.

But it's different today.

Brandi's here.

I heard her tell Mrs. Holt that her mom has gotten a job.

That means she's going to be here from now on.

When she walked into the room, I smiled at her . . . a kind of friendly-but-not-too-friendly smile. I, Amber Brown, have decided not to worry so much about making a new best friend, even though I really want one.

So I gave her just a normal smile that you give to the people in your classroom . . . not a please-oh-please-be-my-best-friend smile.

She nodded, looked around the room, and saw that we are the only two fourth graders in the room.

And then she sat down next to me.

There's a loud noise coming from the other side of the room.

Three of the fifth-grade boys are pretending to be Karate masters, chopping at the air, and making noises like "Hi Ya!" (not the hello, "Hi Ya," but the Karate "Hi Ya."

The teacher makes them sit down.

In fact, she makes everyone sit down, and then yells, "Put your heads on your desks!"

I start to laugh.

I try not to, but I can't help it.

"Would you mind sharing with the rest of the group what is so funny, Miss Brown?" the teacher says in a sarcastic voice.

I can't help it if when she said "Put your heads on the desk" I wanted to say, "I can't. It's still attached to my shoulders."

She looks at me.

I think about how my parents are always telling me that I'm going to need a good education to get ahead . . . and I wonder how am I going to get a head if I have to put it on the desk.

I just can't stop laughing.

I try, but once I start, I can't stop.

"You have detention." The teacher walks up to me. "Put your head down, right now."

I do.

Somehow when you have to stay after school every day, it's kind of hard to worry about getting detention.

I keep my head on the desk and think about how, if Justin were here, I could put my sweater over my head and pretend that I had no head.

I look over at Brandi.

She raises one eyebrow, and then bites her lip to keep from laughing.

I put the sweater over my head and pretend that I have no head.

She sort of explodes with laughter.

That makes me laugh more.

It also gets me another day of detention.

It also gets Brandi a day of detention.

The more I try not to laugh, the more I do.

I just can't stop.

Brandi can't either.

The teacher gets very annoyed.

I get a third day of detention, and then a fourth.

Brandi gets a second and third day of detention.

I sit there thinking about my FOUR days of detention.

Once more, Amber Brown Goes Fourth.

Chapter Ten

"Burp."

"Burp."

"Burp."

"Burp."

Then there's a moment of silence.

"Forty. . . . . Don't stop now." Jimmy
and Bobby cheer for Fredrich. "You're almost there . . . . just three more and you'll
beat the record."

"No more." Fredrich pounds his chest.
"There's nothing left. I'm too pooped to
burp."

"Next," Jimmy calls out, holding up the

mermaid. "Who is going to be next? Who is going to win this beauteous mermaid?"

I look at the mermaid—blonde hair, blue plastic body and tail. She has a jewel in her stomach.

Jimmy touches the mermaid's jewel and this weird music comes out.

The mermaid is so ugly.

The music is so out of tune.

I want that mermaid.

I raise my hand.

"Amber Brown," Jimmy calls out. "It's your turn."

I walk up.

And burp.

And burp.

And burp.

Naomi and Alicia start doing burp cheers for me.

Twenty-nine burps . . . . not enough, but I'm getting better.

Yesterday it was twenty-six.

"You're such a lady . . . . NOT," Hannah sneers at me.

I say, "Thank you."

"Immature baby," she adds.

I curtsy.

"Gas bag," she says.

I burp at Hannah.

Just one burp . . . . . but it's a good one.

Hannah walks away.

"Round fifteen to Amber." Gregory is keeping track.

The burping competition ends for the day.

Only one more week until someone wins the mermaid.

Brandi is standing nearby.

I look at her and smile.

Brandi comes up to me, grins, and raises one eyebrow. "Good work, Amber. You may just become Burp Queen of the fourth grade."

I grin back. "Thank you, but it's going to be hard to win. I'm not allowed to practice in Elementary Extension or in detention and my mom has outlawed burping in the house. She says it's disgusting and she got mad when I burped at her instead of saying hello. I need more practice to win the mermaid."

"Her Burpness." Brandi giggles and then says, "You know, if I could burp not by accident, I would join the competition. I really like that dumb mermaid, too."

I think for a minute and then say, "Listen. If I win her, we can share custody. I'll keep her one week and you get her the next."

Brandi looks at me. "That's really nice of you."

I smile.

She says nothing, looking like she's making a big decision, and then says, "Listen. You can come to my house after school to practice. I'll be your burp coach . . . and I'll even braid your hair, if you would like."

"I would like." I grin a humongous grin.

"We'll tell our moms tonight and then you can come over tomorrow," she says.

I can't wait.

Chapter Eleven

Dear Justin

Thanks for writing to me.
I wish you were here. (You probably wouldn't like being here because I'm in detention . . . which I got because I kind of lost my head in Elementary Extension.)

Oh, I added the used gum you mailed me to our gum ball. It was a good idea to put a wet paper towel around it and put it in a baggie (it did leak a little).

I'll keep adding to the ball too. I just wish that you could add the gum yourself.

I also wish your handwriting was better.

I wish to ask you a few questions about your new school's lunch menus (since it's so hard to read your handwriting):

Do they serve worm rolls? Or warm rolls?

Did you really have to eat pimpled feets? Or was it pickled beets? (Either one sounds really gross!)

Do the kids at your school really call the cafeteria hamburger that? Wow!

I have another question. . . . Do they teach penmanship at your new school?

I have another question. Since you are living down south now, are you going to start talking funny? Are you going to think that I talk funny?

It's too bad you aren't here. Jimmy and Bobby are having a burping contest!!!! You should see the prize!!!!!!

Well . . . . here's some more news:

1. My mother's going out with this guy named Max. Secretly, I think of him as Min . . . . . like in minimum. I haven't met him yet . . . . and I really don't want to meet him either.
2. I wish my father would move back.
3. You, too. . . .
4. I've learned to snap my fingers.

5. Oh, you know what? I'm becoming friends with Brandi Colwin. She's really nice. . . . You'd like her.

I hope that you have a new friend too. (Just don't like him or her more than you like me.)

Your friend,

amber

P.S. Don't eat too many worm rolls.

"Brandi," the Elementary Extension teacher says sweetly, "your mother is here to pick up you and Amber."

It's interesting how some teachers get this really sweet voice when parents are around.

I'm so glad that Mrs. Holt uses her sweet voice with her students, not just with the parents.

As we grab our books, I whisper to Brandi, "I hope your mom is very strong."

"Why?" she whispers back.

"Well, she's PICKING us up." I grin.

We both start to laugh . . . . . a lot, but we don't get detention. . . . I think that's because Mrs. Colwin is standing there waiting . . . . . or maybe the teacher is in a better mood.

I know that I'm in a great mood.

Not only am I going over to Brandi's house, but I'm getting my hair braided.

It's going to be Amber Brown's new look.

Chapter Twelve

"Want to see something really gross?" Brandi giggles as we sit in her bedroom.

I nod.

She goes over to her dresser, opens the top drawer, and pulls out a roll of six-foot-long bubble-gum tape.

"Am I allowed to say something about Justin?" I ask, a little afraid that she'll get mad again.

She nods. "As long as you don't compare us . . . . . or make me feel like I just got picked for the 'friend team' because there is no one else left."

"I don't feel that way." I cross my heart. "I promise."

"Good." She opens up the bubble-gum package.

"I don't think that gum is gross. . . . Justin and I always used to buy those and split it . . . . . three feet each. Sometimes we each put half of it in our mouths . . . . . and then when we were all done with it, we added it to this huge chewing-gum ball. I still have the ball. I'll show it to you sometime."

"Cool." Brandi grins and raises one eyebrow.

Ever since the first time she did that, I've

been practicing, but my eyebrow just won't move. My lip goes up instead.

She says, "Yeah . . . . . but did you or Justin ever blow bubble-gum bubbles with your nose?"

I shake my head no.

She grins and takes a long piece of gum, starts chewing, and then when enough is chewed, she takes the wad out of her mouth and smushes it over and around her nose.

Then she breaths out.

It's the most gigantic bubble I have ever seen.

I, Amber Brown, am very impressed.

I try, but realize that before attempting this trick, a person should blow her nose and get rid of the snot first.

I throw my gum out.

It's too disgusting to add to the gum ball.

"Now." Brandi takes out a box. "Let's do the hair weaving."

I sit down on a chair.

"Sit still," Brandi says, handing me a mirror. "You can watch what I'm doing. Just don't move."

I move.

It's very hard for me to sit still.

"Stop wiggling." Brandi puts a piece of cardboard around a small clump of my hair.

I hold up the mirror so I can watch what she is doing.

She holds up lots of different colors of embroidery threads. "Pick out seven colors."

Glitter purple. Glitter pink. Glitter silver. Black. Turquoise. White. Green.

She puts the threads at the top of the braid and starts twisting it around the hair, working with one color at a time, then making patterns on some sections with a second color.

"Don't move. This has to be really tight."

"Where did you learn this?" I ask.

"This summer, when we went to visit California, my cousin Daniela did my hair.

And then she taught me how to do it. We practiced a lot on her old Barbie dolls . . . . and on her dog."

She finishes one braid.

I look in the mirror. "It's terrific."

She continues.

"Brandi." I ask her the question that I've been wanting to ask her ever since she got back. "How come you and Hannah aren't friends anymore?"

She stops braiding for a minute.

"You don't have to answer if you don't want to," I say, even though I really do want her to answer.

She starts braiding my hair again and says nothing.

I don't say anything either.

Finally, she says, "Look. I'll tell you. It's not such a big deal. But I want you to promise not to say anything to anyone else."

"Okay," I promise, and wait for her to begin.

Chapter
Thirteen

Brandi continues to braid my hair as she begins to tell her story.

"When I moved here last year, it was really hard for me." She sighs.

"Everyone already had best friends . . . everyone here already knew each other . . . . and the people who already knew each other didn't have a lot of time for a new person."

"But you were always invited to parties and stuff." I put down the mirror and look at her.

She nods. "But that's not the day-to-day

stuff, telling each other secrets, just hanging out and having a good time . . . . the way that you and Justin did. Sometimes I looked at you and Justin and felt really bad. Where I used to live, I had this friend, Sandy . . . and we were a lot like you and Justin. The two of you looked like you were having so much fun, except for when you had that big fight just before he moved away."

"That was a bad fight." I remember.

"Even though I know it wasn't right, I was glad that you two were fighting." She pulls a little tight on my braid. "I figured that maybe it would give us a chance to be friends. But then you two made up. When Justin moved away, I thought we could get to know each other better. But you went to England . . . and then I was away when you came back."

"Why didn't you just say something?" I jump a little as she pulls on my hair.

"It's not that easy." She shrugs.

I know how she feels.

She continues, "And you two just didn't have room for another good friend. . . . The only person who did was Hannah."

I want to say, "Yeah, because no one else wants to be her friend because she's so bossy," but I don't.

Brandi adds beads to the braid. "So I was friends with Hannah, but it was hard. She's really bossy. Everything's got to be her way. And sometimes she says really mean things."

"I know."

Brandi sits down on the bed and looks at me. "But it was so hard not having a best friend, so I tried to be friends with Hannah. I stayed with her family for a week at the shore. She was really mean to me, saying things like, 'No one else would be your friend.' It got so bad that I called my parents and they came down and picked me up early. Then when my parents and I went to California for a while, I got to spend some time with my cousin, Daniela. She's fifteen and she's really nice. We talked about a lot of stuff. It made me feel better. Then when school started, I thought we could be friends, but it was like you wanted another Justin around, not me, Brandi."

Brandi looks sad.

"But I always thought you were nice. I didn't know you felt so bad." I look at her.

Softly, she says, "Well, I did."

Poor Brandi.

I didn't know that she felt that way, but now I really do know how she felt.

I say, "Brandi, I'm sorry you felt so bad. I'd really like it if we can be friends."

"Me too." She gets up and starts my second braid.

"And not just because Justin moved away."

"Thanks." She tickles my nose with my hair. "And I want to be friends with you not just because I moved away from Sandy."

I think about how Brandi and I do different things than Justin and I did.

Somehow I don't think that hair braiding
is something he would be interested in.

And Brandi likes to read books more than
he did.

And she talks about how she feels. That's
not something that Justin likes to do.

I do miss him a lot though.

There will never be another Justin.

But there would never be another
Brandi, either.

Brandi says, "If some new kids move
here, let's be nice to them, even if we do
become best friends."

I nod and think about all of the kids who
have best friends move away. I think about
all of the kids who have to move away.

I bet it's hard for all of them.

I wonder if it's hard for grownups when
their friends move away.

I think about how Justin's mom was my

mother's friend, and she moved away . . . . and how my dad moved away . . . . and even though my mom and dad were definitely not best friends when they split up, I wonder if my mom needs a new best friend too.

I wonder if Max is that new friend. It's not something easy for me to think about right now.

Brandi finishes the second braid.

I think about how she said we might become best friends.

I guess that's something that doesn't always happen right away . . . by snapping your fingers.

Oh, well, I learned to snap my fingers. . . . It just took practice. So I, Amber Brown, can learn how to be a best friend. . . .

Thwip . . . snap . . . I hope.

Brandi hands me the mirror. The two braids look wonderful.

"I love them," I say.

Then I pretend to stick the bead up my nose, even though I don't really do it because I know it could be dangerous.

"Perfect in every way." I continue, "Now, let's practice the burping. I really want us to win that mermaid."

Chapter
Fourteen

I press the stone on the mermaid's stomach and she makes her strange sound.

It makes me laugh.

I look at her long, thick blonde hair and wonder if Brandi and I should give her braids, with thread and beads, too.

I wonder what Gregory Gifford is doing with his mermaid, the burping trophy one.

That boy burped ninety-two times to win it.

Then he burped the alphabet.

He is definitely the Burp Champion of our school, if not the whole world.

I didn't even come close to his score.

I burped thirty times and then I got the hiccups.

When Gregory got the mermaid, he pretended she was Karate Mermaid and had her make chopping motions at all of the boys.

Then he drop-kicked her and the boys played touch football with her.

I really wanted that mermaid.

When I got home, I told my mom that I'd lost.

She didn't seem too upset and said that she hoped that now my burping days were over.

I burped at her.

And then that was it . . . . until now.

She's just given me a present and I've opened it . . . . . and it's the mermaid.

I'm so excited.

Wait until I tell Brandi.

It's going to be such a fun, friend, sharing thing.

"Thanks, Mom." I grin at her. "You're the best."

"Read the card," she says softly.

I read the card.

Your mom said you really
wanted this . . . so I got you
one. I hope you like her.
. . . and I hope that you
like me when we meet.

Max

I put the mermaid down. "I don't want it."

My mother says, "Amber" in a soft, sad voice.

I hate it when she uses that soft, sad voice.

"It's not fair." I make a face. "He's being so nice."

"He *is* so nice." She smiles. "You have no idea how hard it was to find the mermaid. I called Gregory's mom to find out what company made the doll, and then Max called the company to find out where he could buy it . . . . and he called five stores before he found one that had it and would send it to him special delivery."

I look at the mermaid. "It's just a dumb doll. I'm getting too old for dolls anyway . . . . especially for dolls that are bribes."

"Amber." My mother uses that voice again. "Max just wanted to do something that would make you happy . . . . to make me happy . . . . to make all of us happy. And he just wants to meet you."

She looks as sad as her voice sounds.

She looks sad, real sad, not the kind of sad that moms sometimes pretend when they they want to get their kids to do something.

I guess she needs to make new friends, too . . . . . and Max is that new friend. It looks like he's not going away.

I look at the doll and think again about how Brandi is going to laugh when she sees the mermaid . . . . how we'll be able to share it.

I think about how it would have been even better if I had won the other one for burping.

It would have been even better if my dad had gotten the mermaid for me.

But he's in Paris . . . . and I don't think he realized how much I wanted the mermaid.

And then I look at Mom and how sad she is because I wouldn't take the mermaid, and how happy she looked when she talked about how Max got the mermaid for me.

So I pick up the mermaid and say, "I'll write Max a thank-you note."

My mother has me trained to write thank-you notes even though I think it is one of the most boring things in the world to do.

"Maybe someday soon, you'll meet Max," she says.

I start to hand back the mermaid.

"It doesn't have to be right away." She pushes the mermaid back toward me.

"You really like him, don't you." I'm not sure that I want to hear the answer.

She nods. "I do. . . . Amber, life goes on. Things change. We all have to adjust, make new friends, new lives, keep what we can of our old lives . . . the good parts. . . ."

I think about how I've had to do that.

I decide to ask the question that I'm really not sure that I want to hear the answer to. "Are you going to marry Max?"

My mother takes a deep breath. "I'm not sure. It's too soon to know that . . . but truthfully, I do care for him a great deal . . . . a great deal."

Two "a great deals." . . . . This sounds pretty serious.

"So will you meet him?" she asks.

I shrug. "Do I have to? Right now?"

"Not yet . . . . . not if you really don't feel ready, but I would like you to meet him someday . . . . . soon." She looks so serious.

I look at her, at the mermaid, think about my father, and sigh. "Soon . . . not yet though, please. I need to get used to some things first."

When I was little, I thought that things were always going to be the same. Actually, it wasn't even something I thought about . . . . it just always was the same, in all the big ways.

And then it all changed, in all the big ways.

And I hate it.

But I, Amber Brown, can't change it back again to the way it was.

I guess that there will always be changes in my life.

I guess it's like that for everyone.

It's that way for everyone I know—me, Justin, our families, Brandi.

So, I guess that I just have to go on getting used to my new life, my new class . . . . . . Amber Brown Goes Fourth . . . . that's the way it is . . . . . at least, until I get to fifth grade . . . . Then I guess it'll be Amber Brown Takes the Fifth . . . .

But I have a long way to go before that happens.